D1371236

Taylor Elementary Library
2600 N Stuart St.
Arlington, VA   22207

701 706 49
Taylor Elementary Library
2600 N Stuart St.
Arlington, VA   22207

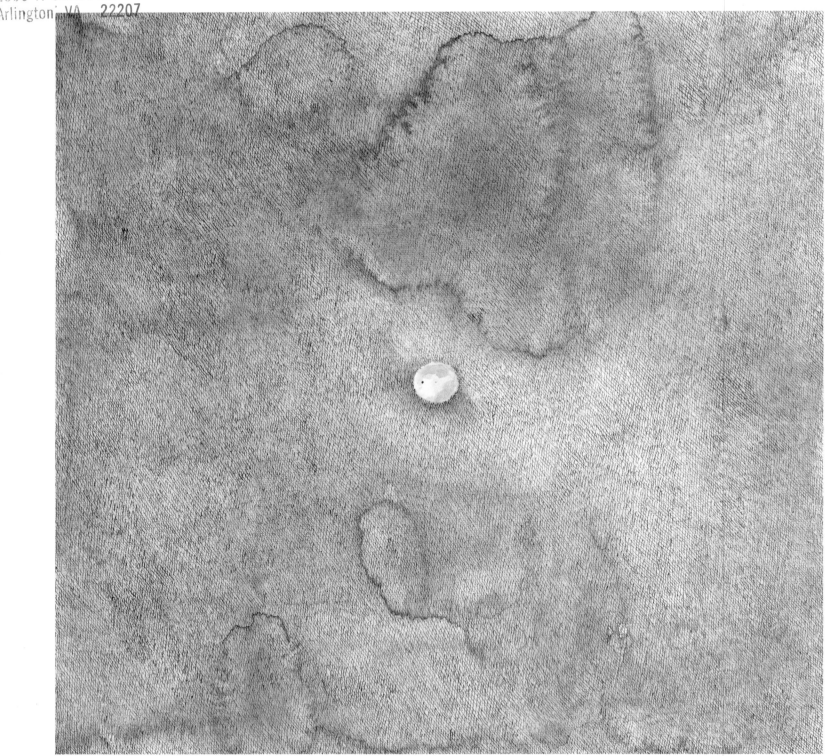

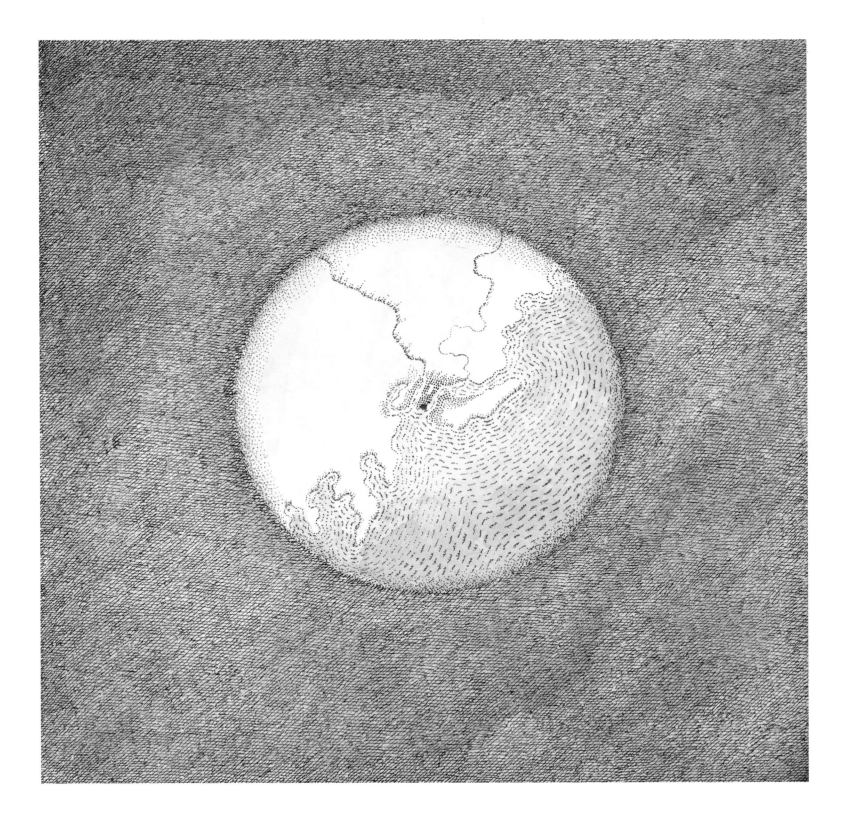

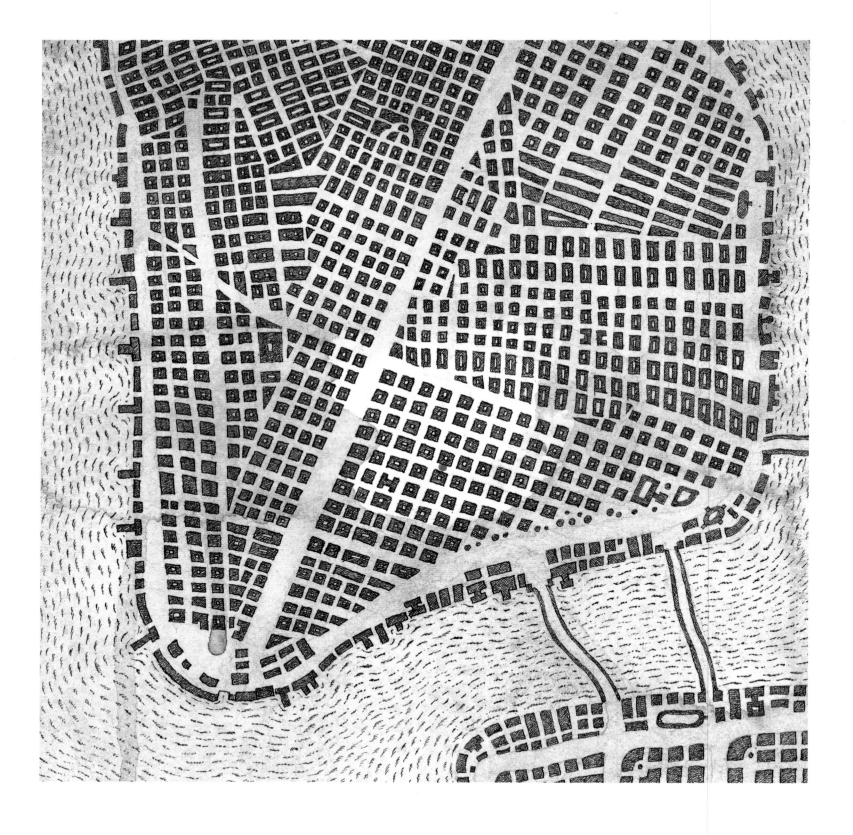

M A D L E N K A

Peter Sís

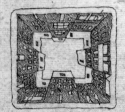

 Square Fish

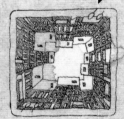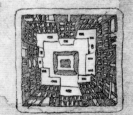

Farrar Straus Giroux • New York

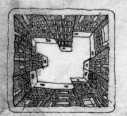

In a country, in a city, on a block, in a house,

In the universe, on a planet, on a continent,

in a window, in the rain, a little girl named

Madlenka

finds out her tooth wiggles.

She has to tell everyone.

Hey, everyone . . . my tooth is loose!

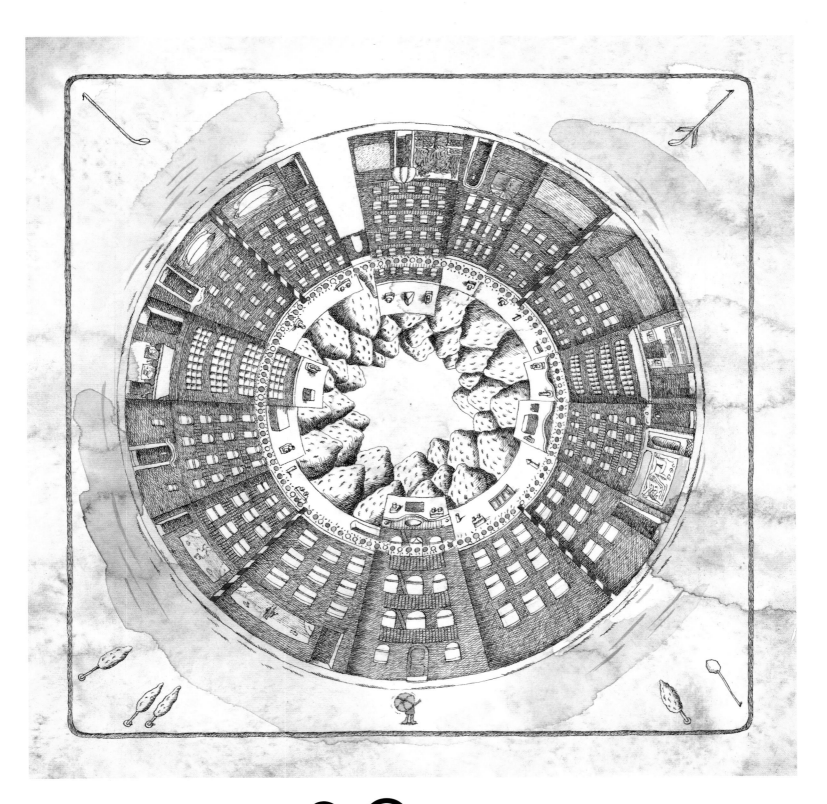

LO O O S E

Jumping with joy, she skips down the street
and sees her friend Mr. Gaston, the French baker.

CROISSANTS

CHOCOLATE CAKES

MADELEINES

 CAKES WITH FRUIT

FRENCH BREAD

WHEN I HAVE
A BIRTHDAY
HE PUTS A PINK
BALLERINA
ON MY CAKE ...→

FINANCIERS

HE TELLS ME ABOUT PARIS

AND ABOUT FRANCE

MR. GASTON BAKES

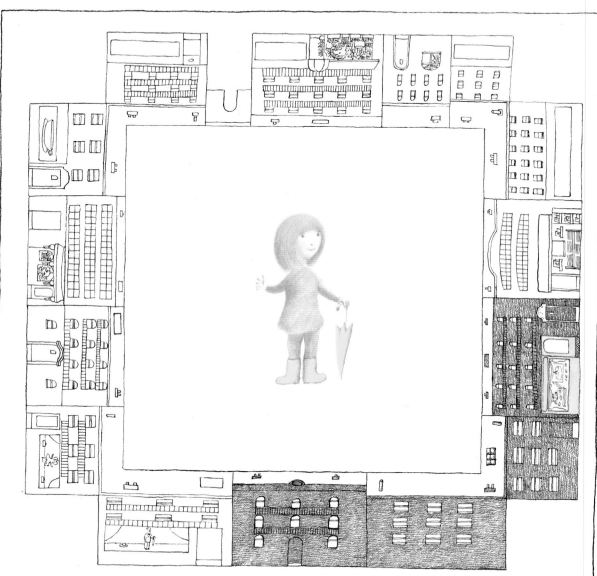

I AM A BIG GIRL NOW

HELLO, MR. GASTON   MY TOOTH IS LOOSE!

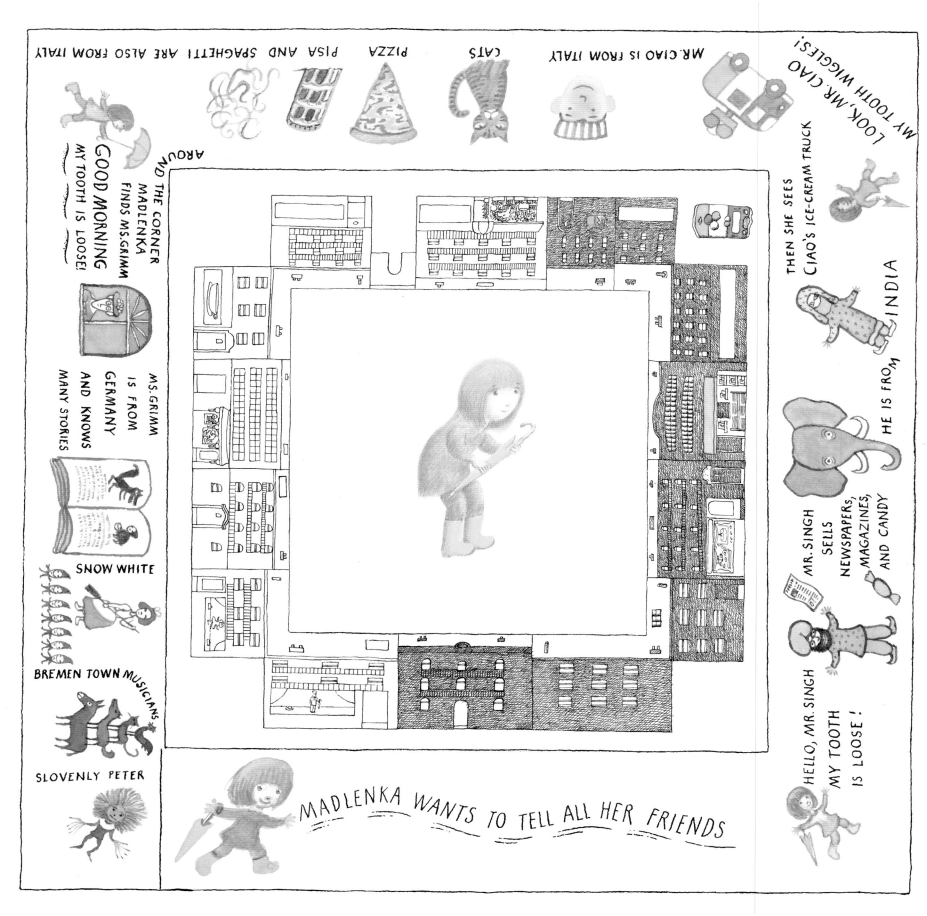

AROUND THE CORNER MADLENKA FINDS MS.GRIMM

PISA AND SPAGHETTI ARE ALSO FROM ITALY

PIZZA

CATS

MR.CIAO IS FROM ITALY

LOOK, MR. CIAO MY TOOTH WIGGLES!

GOOD MORNING MY TOOTH IS LOOSE!

MS.GRIMM IS FROM GERMANY AND KNOWS MANY STORIES

SNOW WHITE

BREMEN TOWN MUSICIANS

SLOVENLY PETER

THEN SHE SEES CIAO'S ICE-CREAM TRUCK

HE IS FROM INDIA

MR. SINGH SELLS NEWSPAPERS, MAGAZINES, AND CANDY

HELLO, MR. SINGH MY TOOTH IS LOOSE!

MADLENKA WANTS TO TELL ALL HER FRIENDS

Buon giorno, Maddalena.
This calls for a treat.

Guten Tag, Magda. Let me tell you a story.

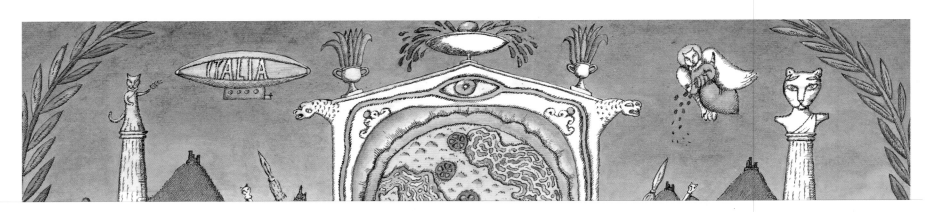

Madlenka thinks this must be the best day of her life.

Oh, there's Mr. Eduardo, the greengrocer.

PYRAMIDS

PEOPLE

RIVERS

MOUNTAINS

LATIN AMERICA ALSO HAS

SNAKES

PARROTS

JAGUARS

BUTTERFLIES

TAPIRS

RAIN

FOREST

EDUARDO ALSO HAS

PINEAPPLES

ORANGES

APPLES

BANANAS

CORN

TOMATOES

POTATOES

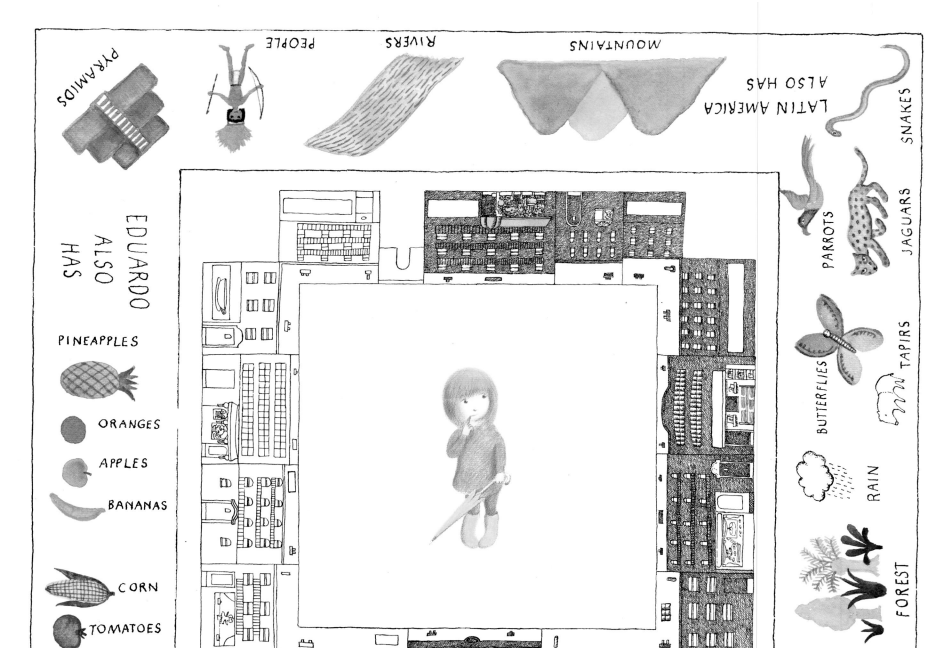

HELLO, EDUARDO

MY TOOTH WIGGLES!

EDUARDO IS FROM LATIN AMERICA

HE SELLS

FLOWERS   TREES   PLANTS

HIS STORE FEELS LIKE A RAIN FOREST

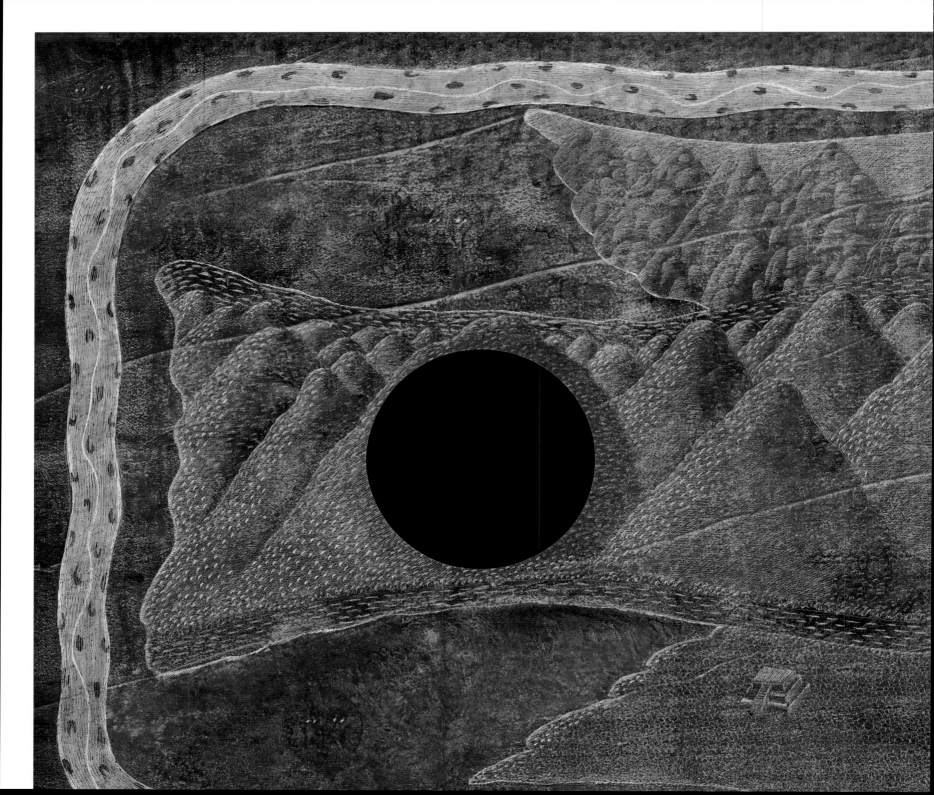

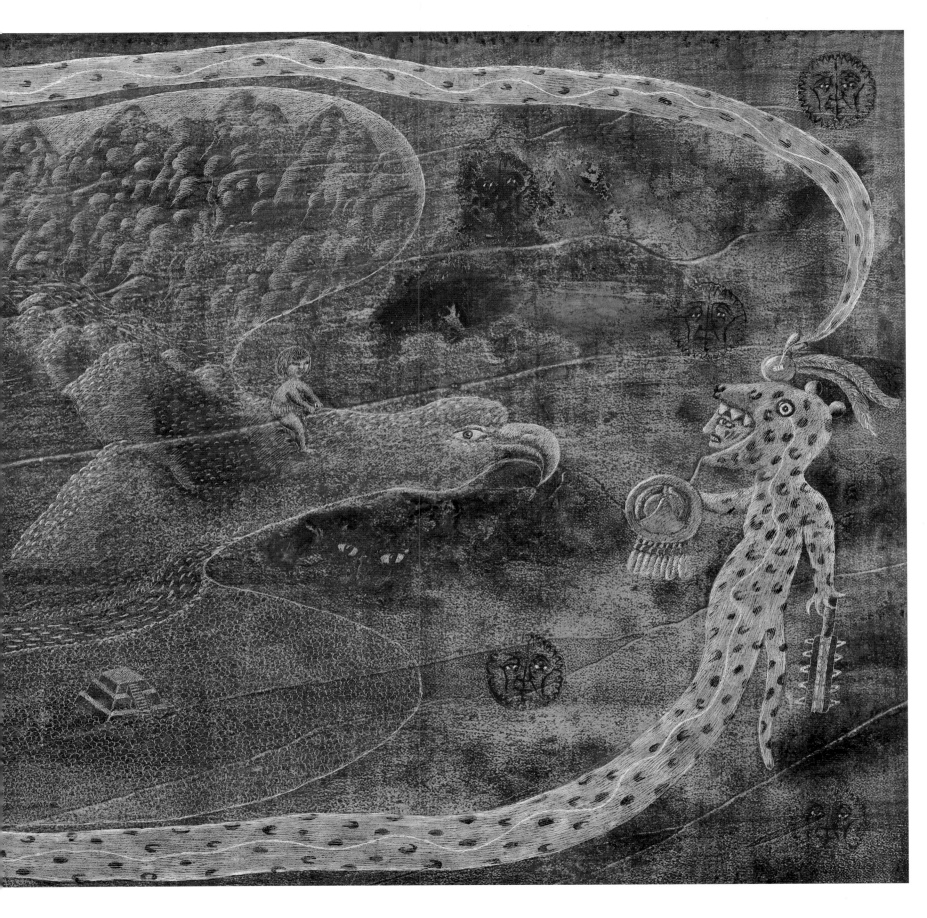

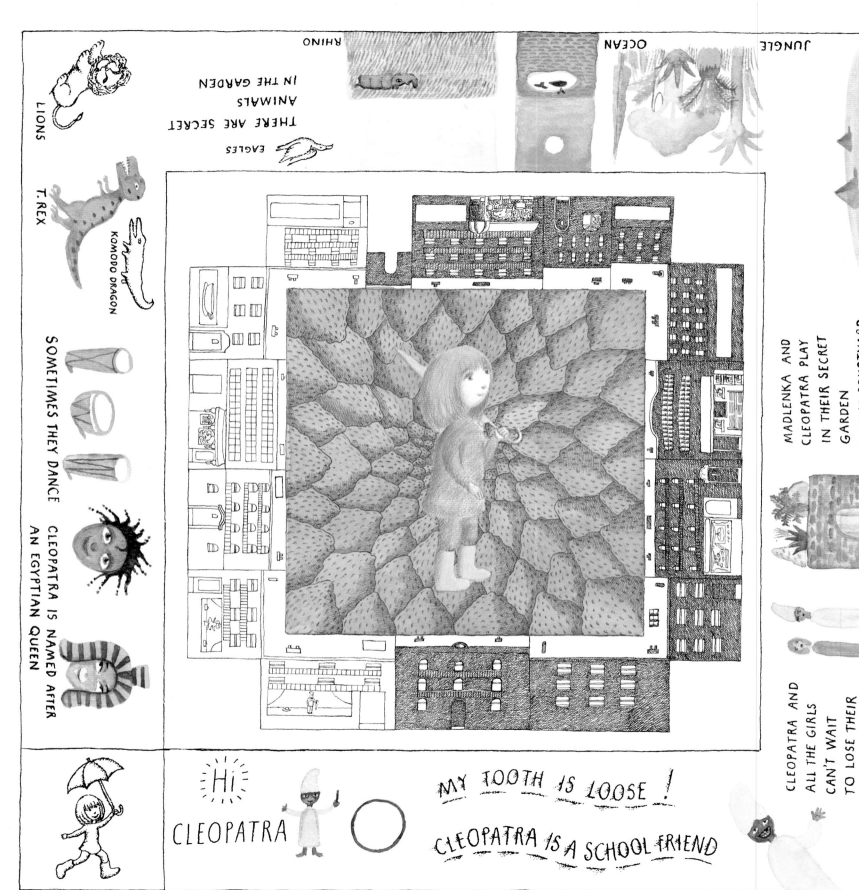

LIONS

T. REX

KOMODO DRAGON

RHINO

OCEAN

JUNGLE

THERE ARE SECRET ANIMALS IN THE GARDEN

EAGLES

THEY PRETEND IT IS DESERT

SOMETIMES THEY DANCE

CLEOPATRA IS NAMED AFTER AN EGYPTIAN QUEEN

MADLENKA AND CLEOPATRA PLAY IN THEIR SECRET GARDEN IN THE COURTYARD

CLEOPATRA AND ALL THE GIRLS CAN'T WAIT TO LOSE THEIR BABY TEETH AND GROW UP....▶

HI

CLEOPATRA

MY TOOTH IS LOOSE!

CLEOPATRA IS A SCHOOL FRIEND

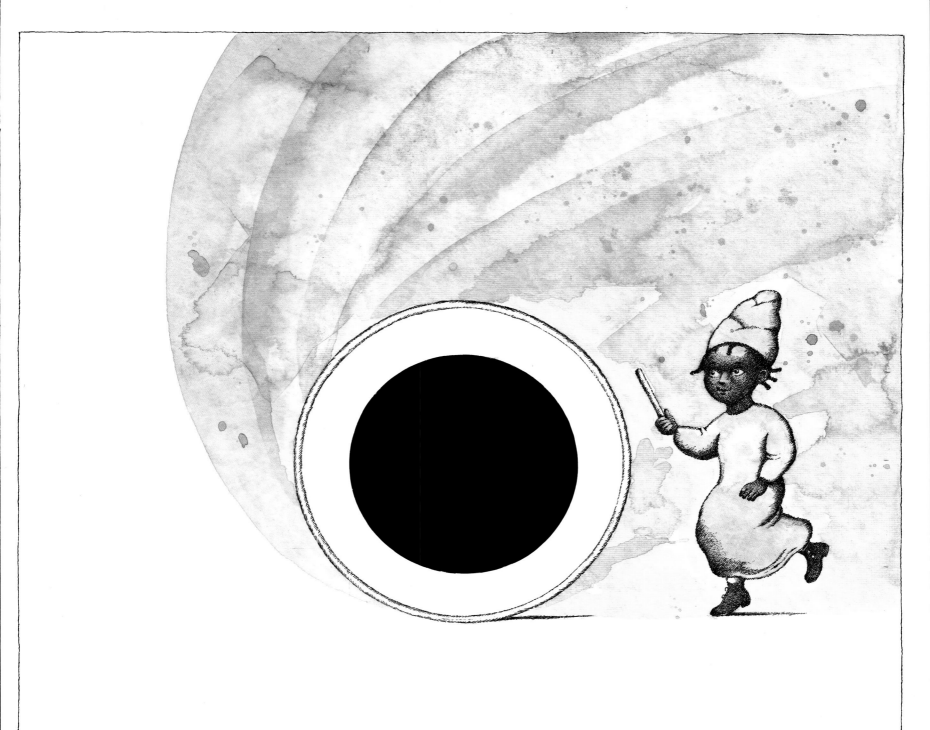

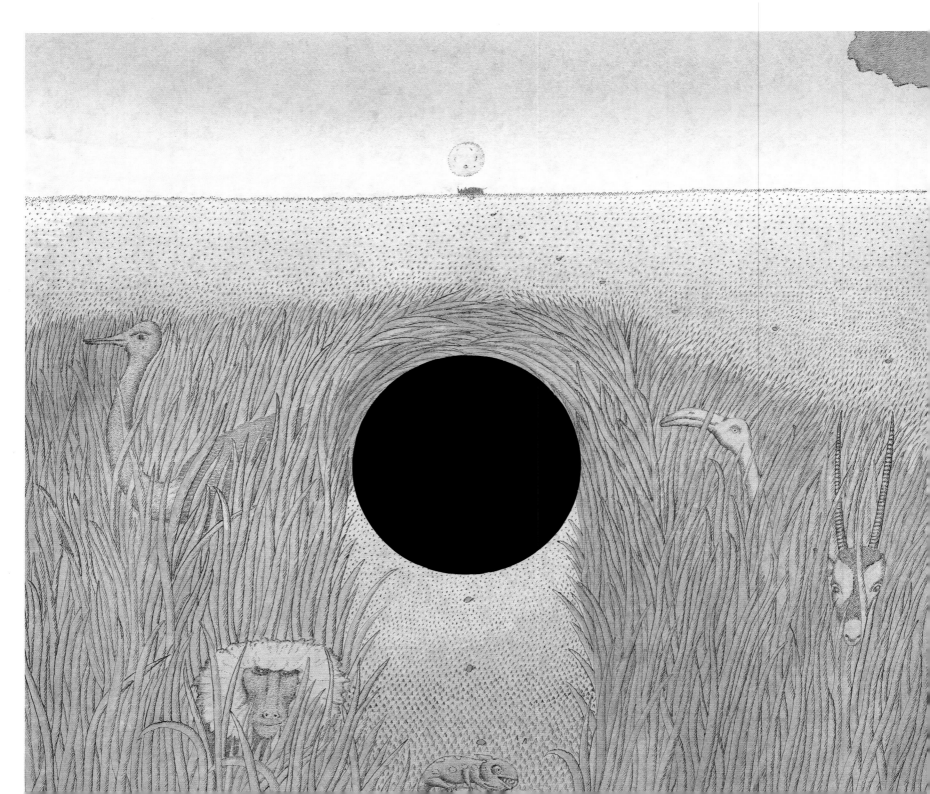

Who else can she tell?

Oh! Mrs. Kham has to know.

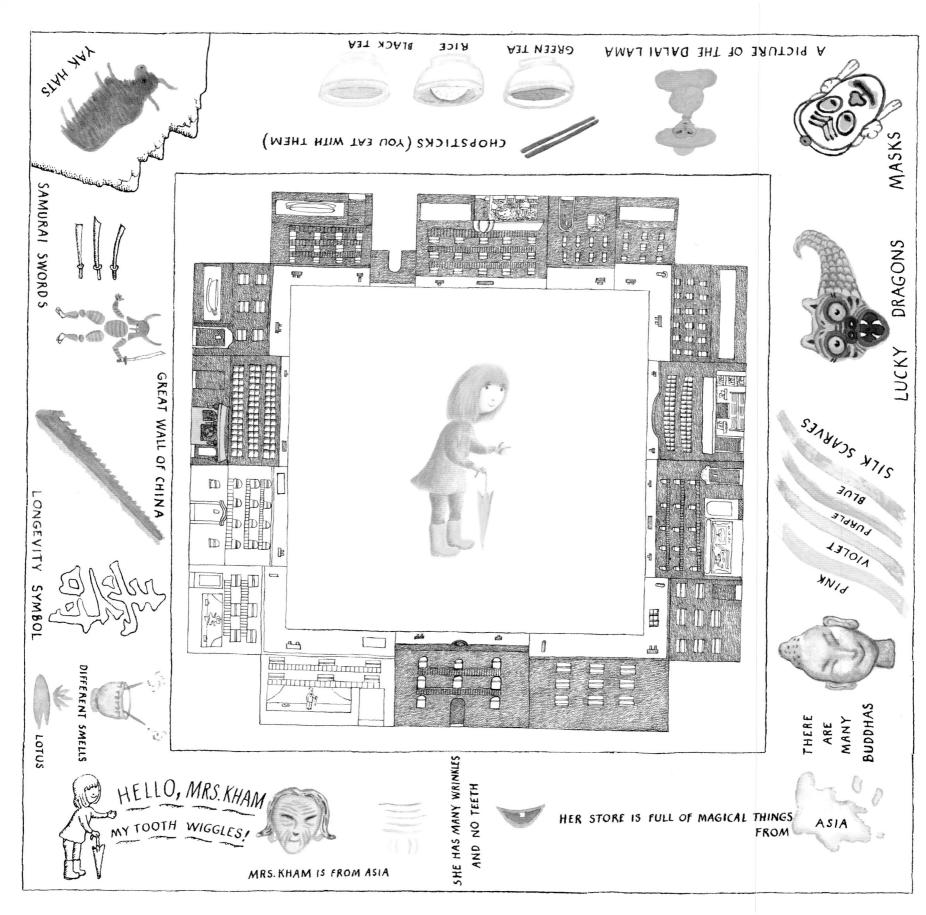

YAK HATS

SAMURAI SWORDS

GREAT WALL OF CHINA

LONGEVITY SYMBOL

DIFFERENT SMELLS

LOTUS

BLACK TEA

RICE

GREEN TEA

CHOPSTICKS (YOU EAT THEM WITH)

A PICTURE OF THE DALAI LAMA

MASKS

LUCKY DRAGONS

SILK SCARVES

BLUE

PURPLE

VIOLET

PINK

THERE ARE MANY BUDDHAS

ASIA

HER STORE IS FULL OF MAGICAL THINGS FROM

SHE HAS MANY WRINKLES AND NO TEETH

MRS. KHAM IS FROM ASIA

HELLO, MRS. KHAM

MY TOOTH WIGGLES!

Oh dear. I'm late.

Madlenka! Where have you been?

Well . . . I went around the world.

And I lost my tooth!

TO TERRY·MADELEINE·MATEJ·ALL BORN IN NEW YORK CITY

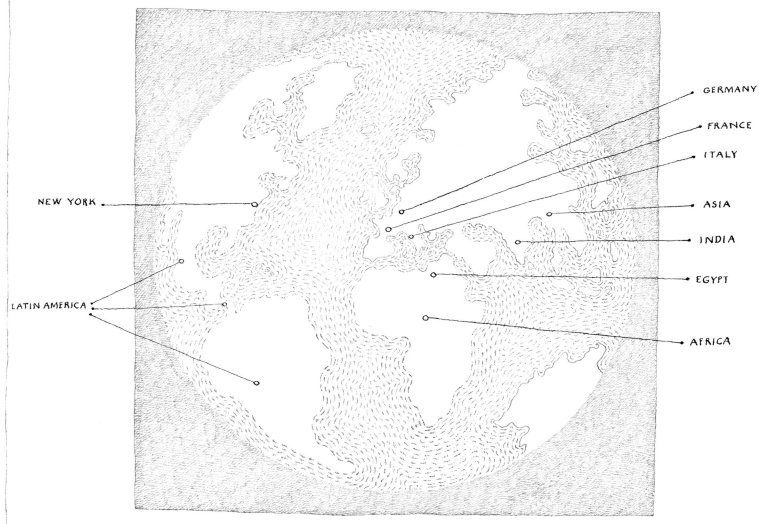

GERMANY

FRANCE

ITALY

ASIA

NEW YORK

INDIA

EGYPT

LATIN AMERICA

AFRICA

SQUARE FISH

An imprint of Macmillan

MADLENKA. Copyright © 2000 by Peter Sís. All rights reserved. Printed in China by South China Printing Co. Ltd.,
Dongguan City, Guangdong Province. For information, address Square Fish, 175 Fifth Avenue, New York, NY 10010.

Square Fish and the Square Fish logo are trademarks of Macmillan and
are used by Farrar, Straus and Giroux under license from Macmillan.

Library of Congress catalog card number: 99-57730
ISBN: 978-0-312-65912-7

Originally published in the United States by Frances Foster Books,
an imprint of Farrar, Straus and Giroux

Square Fish logo designed by Filomena Tuosto
First Square Fish Edition: 2010

10 9 8 7 6 5 4 3 2

mackids.com

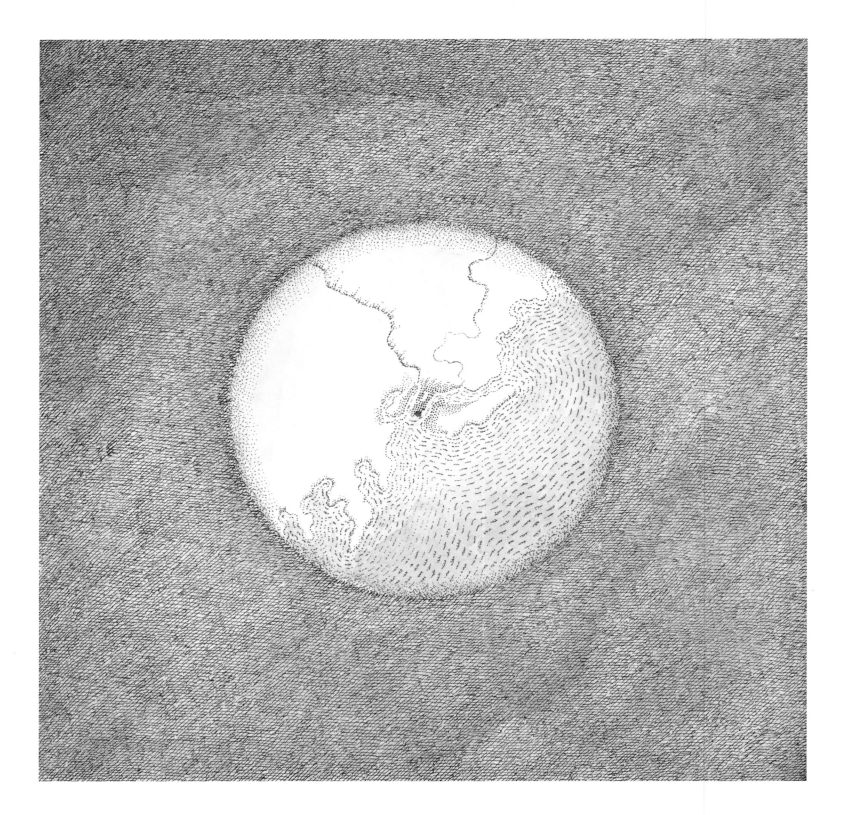

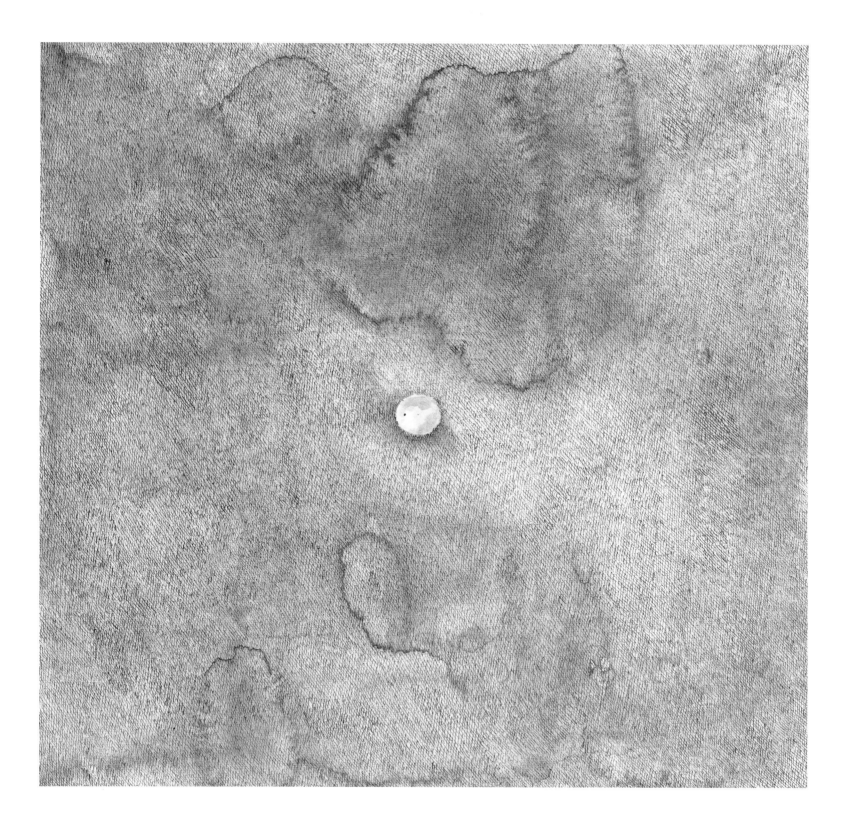

7017 0649

E   Sis, Peter
Sis   Madlenka

TAYLOR ELEM.
ARLINGTON, VA